DREAMWORKS

Spirit

RIDING FREE

Apple Adventure!

Cover design by Ching Chan. Cover illustration by Maine Diaz.

Little, Brown and Company
Hachette Book Group
1290 Avenue of the Americas, New York, NY 10104
Visit us at LBYR.com

First Edition: August 2019

Little, Brown and Company is a division of Hachette Book Group, Inc. The Little, Brown name and logo are trademarks of Hachette Book Group, Inc.

The publisher is not responsible for websites (or their content) that are not owned by the publisher.

Library of Congress Control Number 2019937641

ISBNs: 978-0-316-48745-0 (pbk.), 978-0-316-53684-4 (Scholastic ed.), 978-0-316-48746-7 (ebook)

Printed in the United States of America

LSC-C

Printing 5, 2021

OFFICIAL
MARK OF
SPIRIT

DREAMWORKS
Spirit
RIDING FREE
Apple Adventure!

G. M. Berrow
Illustrated by **Maine Diaz**

Little, Brown and Company
New York Boston

Chapter 1

Lucky Prescott's kitchen was a mess. There were bowls and spoons everywhere, and most of the countertops were covered in flour. She was hosting a "Best Friends Baking Day." Every so often, Lucky, Abigail, and Pru—the PALs—would get together to make all sorts of yummy treats.

Today was special. Abigail wanted to try out some new recipes that she'd invented. Baking was one of her favorite family traditions. Usually the girls would take over the kitchen at the Stone household. But today there had been one problem: Abigail's little brother, Snips, was being really annoying. He kept marching through the kitchen, banging pots and pans with a wooden spoon and asking for a taste of something sweet. It was really interrupting the girls' creative process.

So Lucky had suggested they move to her house. It would be nice and quiet. Especially since her dad, Jim Prescott, had promised to practice his harmonica at the depot from now on.

"Abigail! Pass me that pie tin," said Lucky. She wiped her forehead with the back of her hand. A big smear of flour stayed behind. She didn't care.

"Here ya go!" Abigail chirped. She had already buttered her favorite pie tin. Now all it needed was the crust...and the fruit filling! Today's specialty was blueberry.

The secret ingredient in Abigail's new recipe was a handful of cranberries. She said a splash of tart would bring out the sweet flavor of the blueberries. Lucky wasn't sure about that, but she was excited to taste the new flavor. Cranberries always reminded her of autumn. It was going to be the perfect treat for a crisp day like today.

Pru carefully rolled out the crust with the rolling pin and laid it in the tin just as Abigail had taught her.

"Nice work!" Abigail nodded her approval. It was very easy for the crust to tear. "Now pour in the blueberries."

"I'm on it!" Lucky smiled as she poured the sugary mixture into the shell. "Should we do a lattice top?" On a previous Best

Friends Baking Day, Abigail had shown her friends how to cut strips of dough and weave them together on the top of the pie. It looked really neat.

The girls decided it might be better to try something new. "How about some fall leaves?" Pru rolled out another piece of crust. She stamped a leaf-shaped cookie cutter into it. "Or a horse!"

"*Ooooh*, good idea, Pru." Lucky nodded. She began to look through her cookie cutters for a horse-shaped one. Even though the pie was just for the three of them to enjoy, it was still fun to make it look like a showstopper.

After they'd decorated the top with leaves and horses, the girls popped the pie into the oven to bake. Then all there was left to do was wait. Well, that and the cleaning-up part. It was not their favorite, but when Lucky, Abigail, and Pru worked together, cleanup usually went pretty fast.

But before they could start, Jim Prescott popped his head in. "What's that smell?" He took a long, deep sniff and smiled. "Is it blueberry?"

"We'll save you a slice, Mr. Prescott!" Abigail laughed. "As your payment for letting us ruin your kitchen."

"Seems like a pretty *sweet* deal to me!" Jim gave a thumbs-up. "Well, I'll leave you girls to it, but I just wanted to give you this first. It's addressed to 'The Miradero Herd!'" He held up a crisp white envelope. It had

a gold wax seal with a heart symbol on it.
Lucky recognized that symbol right away.
She darted over and took the letter from
her father's hands.

"It's from the Frontier Fillies!" Lucky exclaimed. She and her friends had recently become a part of the Frontier Fillies, an organization for girls and their horses. Each town had their own group, called a "herd." The Miradero Herd was a little bit newer than some of the others, but they had quickly caught up by earning badges in the Boots and Bows event, the Majestic Mare display, and all sorts of other fun activities at the Frontier Fillies Jamboree that summer.

Lucky held up the envelope. "It's from Ms. Hungerford! Should I open it now?"

"What are you waiting for?" said Pru, then she thought better of it. "Actually, maybe you should wash your hands first."

A blueberry covered in sugar syrup ran down Lucky's wrist. She licked it off. Aunt Cora was always reminding Lucky to wash her hands.

"Oh yeah. Good point." Once Lucky had washed up, she carefully lifted the golden seal and read aloud. "Kind salutations to the current holders of the Hungerford Heart—the Miradero Herd!"

Pru and Abigail smiled with pride.

The three of them had worked very hard to win the coveted prize at the Jamboree. Snips had almost messed up their chances when he'd tried to sabotage the other herds' turns during the events. But it had all worked out in the end. The other herds had voted for Miradero to win because they had displayed the four qualities that represented the award: honor, compassion, valor, and honesty.

Lucky continued reading: "I am pleased to inform you that we have decided to hold the first-ever Frontier Fillies Winter Jamboree! There will be winter trail rides, log cabins, and of course...the chance to earn more badges." Lucky felt her heartbeat quicken. She loved earning badges and sewing them onto her sash.

"Wow!" Abigail clapped her hands. "That sounds so fun! I bet Boomerang would love a winter trip. Just imagine it—trotting through the snowy woods....*Oooh!* We could make a snow-horse!"

Pru nodded. "We obviously have to go."

"Obviously!" Abigail echoed.

But there was more. Lucky kept reading. "To get the first event off the ground, each herd will have to plan a fund-raiser. The herd with the most contributions to the Winter Jamboree will win a special prize—the Golden Horseshoe Trophy!"

"*Ooooooh...*" the girls said in unison. A trophy? They were definitely intrigued.

"I wonder how many karats are in the Golden Horseshoe Trophy," Abigail joked. "Get it? Because horses love carrots!" The girls giggled, each imagining placing the trophy on a special shelf in

the barn. It would look so wonderful! Of course, they had to actually win it first. It would be amazing to be the holders of the Hungerford Heart *and* to be the first-ever winners of the Golden Horseshoe. It would prove how great the PALs were at being Frontier Fillies and at being a team! Now all they had to do was clean the kitchen, *and* come up with an award-winning fund-raiser! Lucky just hoped it would be a piece of cake...or pie!

Chapter 2

Lucky shivered as she and the girls opened the barn door. The seasons were definitely changing. Good thing Spirit had wanted to visit Chica Linda and Boomerang in the barn, where it was a little warmer. It would also be easier to tell the horses the good news about the Winter Jamboree, since they were all together. Maybe they already knew! Lucky often wondered if the horses talked about the girls in horse-speak when they were gone. Probably not, but it was a funny thought.

Abigail skipped forward to Boomerang's stall and opened the door. "You look so dapper in your new blanket, Boomerang. Is it warm?" The brown-and-white American Paint Horse whinnied. That meant he liked his new blanket very much.

Next to him was Pru's Palomino horse, Chica Linda. She poked out her head from her stall. Chica Linda leaned down and nuzzled Pru, then sniffed her pockets for treats. Luckily, each girl had remembered to bring a handful of Abigail's special oat biscuits with them. "Hungry today, huh, girl?" Pru asked as Chica Linda ate three of them in one bite. She took that as a yes.

"We were, too." Abigail patted her stomach. Each girl had eaten a big slice of the cran-blueberry pie. Abigail had been right—the cranberries had been the perfect touch! They'd saved the rest of the pie for Mr. and Mrs. Prescott. The girls hadn't wanted to get tummyaches.

"How does a trail ride sound to you guys?" Lucky asked, petting Spirit's soft light-brown hide. "I want to see all the leaves changing color."

"My dad calls that 'leaf-peeping,'" said Abigail. She unhooked Boomerang's saddle and bridle from the wall. "Sounds pretty silly, doesn't it? *Peep! Peep!*"

Lucky and Pru agreed, but it didn't stop them from wanting to go.

After Chica Linda and Boomerang were tacked and ready, the girls mounted their horses. Lucky never rode Spirit with a saddle, because he was actually a wild and free horse. The two of them had their own special way of doing things. Lucky liked it that way. Spirit leaned down so she could lift herself up onto his sturdy back. Lucky grabbed on to his mane.

"To the leaf-peeping!" Abigail laughed and pointed ahead. Then they took off toward their favorite trail at a slow trot.

It was only a few minutes before Lucky's thoughts drifted back to the Winter Jamboree fund-raiser. She really wanted to win the Golden Horseshoe to add to her herd's trophy collection. With how well

the three of them worked together, they
had to win, right? All they needed was
the perfect idea to clinch the competition.
Riding on the open trail always gave her
lots to think about. Something about the
fresh air and the wind in her face made her
feel invigorated. It was the perfect time to

be brilliant. "We should try to brainstorm some ideas for the fund-raiser while we ride!"

"*Hmmm...*" Pru squinted, which was her "thinking face." "Why don't we put on a show? We can sell tons of tickets. That ought to give us a good shot at raising the most funds."

"What kind of show?" Abigail asked. The girls steered their horses through the trees and along the stream. Boomerang bent down and took a drink. "Like a puppet show? I think Maricela has an old wooden puppet theater. Maybe she'd lend it to us."

"No, I was thinking more like a horse showcase, kinda like we did at the last Jamboree," Pru replied. She trotted ahead and jumped Chica Linda over a log. The mare soared through the air and landed gracefully, her hooves thudding on the soft earth. "Stuff like that!" Pru looked proud. Though they had always been good at jumping, she and Chica Linda were constantly getting better and jumping even higher. It took a lot of practice.

"But do you really think we'd sell enough tickets to win the Golden Horseshoe?" Lucky wondered. Performance was in their blood, especially after the time they'd all run away to join the circus, El Circo Dos Grillos. But that had been a while ago. They might all be a bit rusty. Plus, Miradero was a pretty small town. "We might need to do the show a few times to sell enough. Do you think people would come to the show more than once?"

"I'm not sure...." Pru shrugged. "Maybe if we practice some new, impressive tricks? We can try different things at each show!"

"Let's see what we can do!" Abigail replied. She had been itching to learn some new stuff with Boomerang.

For the next hour, Lucky, Abigail, and Pru took turns trotting ahead on the trail and surprising one another with random tricks. Pru and Chica Linda did an elegant dressage dance, weaving through a row of trees while the other girls sang a song and clapped a beat.

Abigail and Boomerang did a silly comedy routine where they pretended to

tightrope walk. Abigail got Boomerang
to rear back on his hind legs, and then
he carefully walked across a bridge in a
perfectly straight line, one hoof in front of
the other. It took quite a long time for them
to get to the other side, because Abigail
kept bursting into fits of giggles.

And last but not least, Lucky tried
to impress her friends by jumping onto
Spirit's back from a tree branch.

"Ta-da!" Lucky laughed as she landed
perfectly on Spirit's back. A shower of
crunchy, orange leaves fell on them from
the shaking branch above her. A few
stuck in her hair, but Lucky didn't mind.
She was doing her favorite activity in the
world—riding horses with her best friends.

Pru and Abigail clapped and whistled in appreciation. Lucky stayed standing on Spirit's back and made a little bow to her adoring fans.

By the time they'd finished doing tricks, the PALs had completely forgotten why they'd started in the first place. Lucky looked up and noticed that the landscape around them had changed. The trees were much thicker than on their normal route. The colors of the leaves were brilliant hues of red, orange, and yellow. It was almost as if they were on fire. It was excellent leaf-peeping, but the girls were a little surprised that they'd gotten so distracted. They'd only meant to go for a short ride.

"I think we must have taken the Crested

Ridge trail instead of our normal route!"
Pru bit her lip. "Chica Linda, what do you
think?" The horse replied with a snort. That
meant yes.

Lucky laid out the options. "We can keep
going for a little bit until we get to the spot
where the trails meet again...or we can turn
back around."

After a short discussion, the girls all
agreed that it would actually be fun to go
a little farther today. They loved learning
about every trail around Miradero. They
had just started off again when Lucky
stopped Spirit and called out to the gang.
"Look! I think I see something up ahead!"

It was a beautiful apple orchard. The
trees were all planted in perfect rows and

were bursting with juicy apples. Lucky didn't even have time to discuss what to do before Spirit took off in the direction of the grove. All Lucky could do was hold on tight and hope her friends followed.

Chapter 3

Once Spirit reached the edge of the orchard, he found a little pile of fallen fruits and helped himself to it. The horse immediately scarfed down six Honeycrisp apples and even rolled a few over to Chica Linda and Boomerang. The three horses crunched and neighed happily.

Lucky, Pru, and Abigail couldn't help laughing at their goofy horses. It was fun to watch them playing around, but they knew they should probably stay for only a few minutes. They still had a long ride home, and Lucky was starting to get quite thirsty and hungry. But as Spirit crunched down on another apple, Lucky decided she couldn't wait to go home for food.

"Let's go inside the orchard," whispered Lucky. Her tummy rumbled. That slice of pie seemed like an awfully long time ago. "Maybe we can buy a few apples for a snack." She pointed to the apple cores the horses had spit out. "And pay for *those*."

"If we can even find someone to pay!" Pru replied. She hopped off Chica Linda's saddle and walked over to look down the row of trees. "There's no one here, Lucky. Do you think we could take just a few apples?"

"Lucky's got the right idea. We shouldn't steal any apples." Abigail was very serious about living by the values of the Hungerford Heart.

"Ugh, I know you're right, but I'm

hungry," Pru admitted. She held her stomach. "We should have packed a few pickle sandwiches for the road."

"Yuck!" Abigail made a face. Pru had really weird taste in food sometimes.

"Don't worry; I'm sure we can take a few apples and find a place to leave our money with a note," Lucky assured her friends. She skipped over to a tree and plucked the most perfect-looking apple from its branch. As Lucky bit into it, her eyes grew wide with amazement. It tasted perfect, too. "Wow, this is the best apple I've ever tasted!"

"¡Gracias!" said an unfamiliar voice. "We grew them ourselves."

The girls spun around. They'd been caught in the act! A girl who looked just a little older than them stood nearby. She had short, curly dark hair and bright-green eyes. Her red sweater made them look even greener. Luckily, she didn't seem mad that the PALs and their horses were there. In fact, she greeted them warmly. "Me llamo Vida! And this is my family's huerto de manzanas."

"That means 'apple orchard,'" said Pru. "I remember it from our Spanish lesson."

"¡Muy bien! Very good!" Vida nodded. She motioned to the apple in Lucky's hand. "Por favor, help yourselves. We have plenty to share."

Abigail was still uneasy. "Are you sure?"

Vida just laughed. "¡Sí! Of course. Here—I'll help. I know where the best ones

are." Vida walked over and placed a little ladder under the tree. She began to reach up and pluck apples from the top. "These apples get the most sun," Vida said. "I think that makes them sweeter!" She tossed the apples to Pru and Abigail.

The girls each took a bite and had the same reaction as Lucky.

"So, what do you think?" Vida asked hopefully.

"They're delicious!" Abigail exclaimed. A little bit of apple juice ran down her chin. "These would be perfect in a cinnamon apple tartlet! Or maybe in a crumbly cobbler..."

"Abigail's our resident baker," Lucky explained as Vida passed her a different variety of apple. "She makes up the recipes, but we all like to help."

"I love baking, too," Vida replied absentmindedly. Lucky could see that she was distracted by something. She kept staring off past the girls. "And I love horses. Are those yours?" So that was it!

"You bet!" Pru nodded. She pointed to each horse as she introduced them. "Boomerang is Abigail's, Chica Linda is mine, and Spirit is technically nobody's... but he and Lucky have a pretty special friendship."

"Wow," breathed Vida. Lucky knew that look—Vida was smitten.

"Do you want to pet them?" Lucky offered. The way the horses were posing made them look extra cute. "They love attention, if you couldn't tell already."

"¡Gracias!" Vida happily obliged, taking turns petting each of the horses and feeding them more apples. "I've always loved horses, but my parents never had them when I was little. I saved up all my money from working on the farm and just bought a horse of my own—Cinnamon. Would you like to meet him?"

"Yes!" the girls said all at once. Meeting new horses was one of their favorite things to do—ever. As Vida led them through the orchard to a stable, she explained that Cinnamon was very shy.

The girls were careful not to spook him as they approached. He had a pale-brown hide and a glossy dark-brown mane. His legs darkened into a deeper brown that met his hooves. Underneath his shy exterior, Cinnamon seemed silly and energetic. Lucky couldn't help thinking how fortunate he was to have a home on an apple orchard. We had snacks as far as the eye could see!

"He's beautiful! Is he an American Quarter Horse?" Pru guessed.

"That's right!" Vida nodded, clearly impressed with Pru's horse-breed knowledge. Lucky smiled. With Vida's love of horses, Lucky knew she would fit right in with the PALs.

"You and Cinnamon should come riding with us," said Lucky. She climbed up onto the fence to reach out and pet Cinnamon's soft muzzle. He whinnied and stepped back. His nerves were kicking in.

Vida's face morphed into a funny expression. Maybe Lucky had read the situation wrong. Vida was a little older than them. She probably didn't want to hang around younger kids.

"Well, I would love to, but...I haven't even gotten to ride him yet, porque..." Vida trailed off. She paused for a moment and then mustered up her courage. "Porque...uh...I never learned how to ride." She blushed with embarrassment. "Isn't that awful? I bought myself a horse that I can't even ride!"

The girls assured her there was nothing to be embarrassed about. They'd all started out as beginners! In fact, they agreed that it was pretty exciting for Vida to have all her horse-riding days ahead of her. Lucky, Abigail, and Pru reminisced about the first times they had ridden their horses. It brought up all sorts of happy memories.

"And pretty soon, you'll want to join a Frontier Fillies herd!" Lucky joked. "It's going to be all horses, all the time. You'll see."

"I'd love to hear some more about this 'Frontier Fillies,'" Vida replied. She jumped down from the stable fence and dusted off her hands. "How about some lunch at the farmhouse while you tell me about it? We have apple pie for dessert...."

There was always room for a new friend and another slice of pie, right?

Chapter 4

After some generous helpings of steaming-hot stew and crusty bread with freshly churned butter, the girls were feeling much better. Vida had introduced them to her mamá and papá, Maria and Julio, and her little brother, Hector. He was about Snips's age and kept running through the house, honking a bicycle horn.

"Aren't little brothers the noisiest?!" Abigail yelled over the commotion.

"Back in Miradero, I've got one myself. His name is Snips!"

"You girls live in Miradero?" Maria asked as she served them each a slice of apple pie. "We used to live there when Vida was pequeña." Maria smiled at the thought. "Does Mr. Winthrop still run the ice cream parlor? They had the best chocolate fudge in the whole West."

"He sure does," Pru replied, licking a crumb off her lip. "Lucky even worked there for a bit. She got to scoop the ice cream."

"Now I see why they call you 'Lucky'!" Vida laughed. She looked off into the distance wistfully. "Miradero is muy bonito."

"It sure is." Julio sighed. "But we bought Rojo Delicioso Orchards, so we had to move out this way," he explained. Julio gave his daughter a loving nudge. "Vida was muy buena about it. She always looks on the bright side."

Vida took a bite of her apple pie and gave a small smile. "I was sad to leave mis amigos at school, but I do love it out here on the farm. And now that I have Cinnamon, it's going to be even better."

If anyone understood what it was like to start over in a new place, it was Lucky.

She was glad she and Vida had so much in common. "I moved to Miradero from the big city not too long ago. It wasn't always easy." Lucky smiled and gestured to Abigail and Pru. "But making some new friends helped a lot. And, of course, getting to ride Spirit made a big difference, too!" Horses were real life changers.

"Wow, Vida, this apple pie is delicious!" said Pru, changing the subject. "What's your secret?"

"Muchas gracias," Vida replied. "It's really all in the apples. Something about the soil in this orchard is special! People always say so."

"Can we buy some apples to bring home?" Abigail asked. She was probably trying to figure out a new recipe that would highlight the unique flavors even more. "I think an orange zest would balance the tartness of the Gala quite nicely."

As soon as the words came out of Abigail's mouth, Lucky had a brilliant idea.

Actually, it was *two* brilliant ideas tied into one. "That's it!" Lucky shouted, and stood up from her chair. Everyone turned their attention to her. "Vida, remember how we told you about the Frontier Fillies?"

"¡Sí!" Vida nodded. She had loved hearing every detail and mentioned how she wished she could join a herd of her own even though she couldn't ride her horse yet.

Lucky smiled. "How would you like to do a trade?"

Vida didn't quite follow Lucky's runaway train of thought. She raised a suspicious eyebrow. "A trade?"

"You should come with us to Miradero. We'll give you riding lessons so that you can learn to ride Cinnamon...in exchange for some crates of your delicious apples! We can use them to hold an apple bake sale for our Frontier Fillies fund-raiser. We'll need the extra pair of hands in the kitchen to make sure we have enough goodies. With your help, we'll definitely win the Golden Horseshoe Trophy! What do you think? Will you come with us?"

"Riding lessons?" Vida's eyes lit up. "An

apple bake sale? That all sounds increíble!" She turned to her parents, looking hopeful. "What do you think? Can I go back to Miradero for a visit and help mis nuevas amigas?"

Maria and Julio exchanged a concerned look and seemed to have a conversation without saying anything. After a moment, Maria's face softened and she smiled at the girls. "I suppose you are old enough to make the trip to Miradero on your own now. And you girls will probably need help bringing all the apples into town. They are quite heavy!"

"You're sure you'll be all right, Vida?" Julio asked, putting his hand on his daughter's shoulder.

"Don't worry, we'll take great care of her! Promise! Vida can stay with me, and we can get started on her lessons right away!"

Lucky practically shouted. She was so happy with how today was turning out. An idea for a fund-raiser *and* a new friend!

Everyone laughed at Lucky's enthusiasm and erupted into excited conversation. Vida was overjoyed by the idea of going back to Miradero, getting to know the PALs, and learning to ride. Hector liked the sound of having the whole playroom to himself. Even Maria and Julio had to admit that the idea of their special Rojo Delicioso apples being featured in Miradero was a good one. They agreed to let Vida go stay at Lucky's house for a few days, provided they heard from Mr. Prescott when she had arrived safely in town.

Lucky felt the excitement bubbling up

inside her. With Vida's help, they would have an extra set of hands *and* an apple expert. They were going to bake the most scrumptious treats ever! Lucky just knew that this arrangement was going to work out perfectly. The Miradero Herd was practically  guaranteed to win the Golden Horseshoe!

"Boomerang! Chica Linda! Spirit!" The girls shouted as they rushed back out to the stable to tell the horses the good news while Vida got ready. Maria and Julio packed up a wagon with a selection of every type of apple that they grew on the orchard.

After taking Vida through her very first lesson in tacking—a fancy way of saying that they put on Cinnamon's bridle and saddle—the girls taught her the correct way to mount and dismount. She was a very fast learner. Even Cinnamon seemed to be coming out of his shell a little bit.

"Let's take it nice and slow, Spirit," said Lucky as she mounted him. Spirit was the most familiar with the landscape because he was a wild horse, so it made sense for them to take the lead.

Abigail looked back over her shoulder. "Are you all right, Vida?" Vida gave her a thumbs-up. "How do the apples look?" The wagon was hitched to Boomerang with a special harness.

"¡Perfecto!" Vida assured her. She promised she would keep a watchful eye on the apples so that none rolled away during the journey. They would need every last

one if they wanted to bake enough treats to raise funds for the Winter Jamboree.

"Are you doing okay, Cinnamon?" Pru added. The horse responded with an excited whinny and scratched his hooves at the dirt. Chica Linda and Boomerang did the same.

"Whoa!" Pru laughed. "Sounds like a *yes* to me!"

The PALs (plus one!) headed back, eager to get started. Lucky had a good feeling about this new bake-sale-and-riding-lessons arrangement. It was a great way to share everything they'd learned as Frontier Fillies with someone new *while* raising funds for the Winter Jamboree! She couldn't wait.

And it might have been Lucky's imagination, but every time she looked back at her friends' horses, she could have sworn their hooves were a shiny, golden color. It was probably just the sunset reflecting off them, but Lucky chose to see it as a good omen. It was a sign of prizes to come—the Golden Horseshoe was within their grasp.

All the Miradero Herd had to do was reach out and pluck it.

Chapter 5

The next day, after Vida settled into the guest room, Lucky called an emergency Miradero Herd meeting in the barn. As soon as the girls entered, the horses began to neigh with delight. Cinnamon looked as if he fit right in with the group, all cozied into the spare stall. He copied Boomerang and Chica Linda, watching the way they nuzzled Pru and Abigail for treats.

"You funny caballo!" Vida said. She brushed his neck with a curry comb. "Of course I have treats for you, too." Cinnamon gobbled them up and showed her his teeth.

"Okay, Fillies!" Lucky held up a colorful sheet of paper. "I called this meeting because I found something amazing at Town Hall."

The Fall Market Festival

"It just looks like an old flyer." Abigail plucked the paper from Lucky's hands and scanned the page. "*The Fall Market Festival,*" she read. She scrunched up her nose. "I don't get it. How is this amazing?"

"It's the perfect place for us to have our bake sale!" Lucky exclaimed. She could just imagine how crowded the market would be. There would be tons of hungry customers in need of delicious apple treats. "Think about it. Lots of people...who want to buy things..."

Pru shook her head. "I don't know, Lucky. Usually the Fall Market Festival has all sorts of apple stuff for sale. How will we stand out in the crowd?"

"With free samples, of course!" Lucky

chirped. She had been thinking about this plan for a few hours now. She had already told Vida her idea and had been met with much enthusiasm. Vida had even made a quick drawing of what the sign on their booth would look like. It had two apples on either side and a golden horseshoe in the middle. Lucky was glad her new friend cared as much as she did.

Abigail raised an eyebrow as she brushed Boomerang. "But how are we supposed to *earn* any money if we give the baked goods away for free?"

"Because we'll have *Rojo Delicioso Orchards* apples," Lucky said proudly. "And no one else at the market will."

"¡Sí! That's true," Vida agreed. "All the

places where we usually sell our apples are much farther north." The other girls considered this. It was a good point, but they were still unconvinced. Lucky wouldn't give up, though. Whenever Lucky focused on a goal, she would stop at nothing to achieve it. Her dad once told her that it was one of her most admirable qualities.

"I just know that once they taste the apples in Abigail's amazing baked goods"—Lucky paced back and forth, throwing her hands up in the air as she spoke—"the customers won't be able to help themselves. They'll *have* to buy something!"

"I think Lucky is right," Pru admitted.

"But there's only one problem...the market is tomorrow afternoon! We'll certainly have our work cut out for us."

"Let's do it," Abigail agreed. "When has the Miradero Herd ever backed down from a challenge?"

"Never!" Lucky cheered. "Golden Horseshoe—watch out!"

The girls spent the rest of the morning mucking out their horses' stalls while Abigail made a big shopping list of all the ingredients they would need. Then they were ready to start their baking extravaganza! So far, they planned to bake apple strudel, apple pie, apple turnovers, apple cider donuts, and a mysterious new recipe called "Apple Abigail."

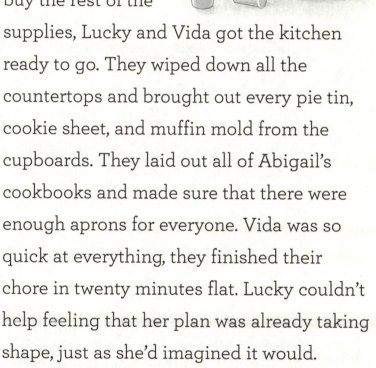

While Pru and Abigail went off with Mr. Granger to buy the rest of the supplies, Lucky and Vida got the kitchen ready to go. They wiped down all the countertops and brought out every pie tin, cookie sheet, and muffin mold from the cupboards. They laid out all of Abigail's cookbooks and made sure that there were enough aprons for everyone. Vida was so quick at everything, they finished their chore in twenty minutes flat. Lucky couldn't help feeling that her plan was already taking shape, just as she'd imagined it would.

"Let's take Cinnamon out for a ride around the stable while we wait for them to get back," suggested Lucky. She could tell Vida was itching to get some horse time in.

"It's as if you read my mind!" Vida's green eyes were bright with excitement.

Vida's lessons were going well. She could already trot Cinnamon around the stable with near-perfect form. She looked happy, her dark curls flowing in the wind behind her. Lucky knew that feeling well. It made her feel warm and fuzzy to get to see Vida experiencing it for the first time.

"Whoa, Cinnamon!" When Vida reached a hurdle, she pulled on Cinnamon's reins as Lucky had taught her. It signaled the horse to come to a stop. They still needed some practice before they tried to do any advanced moves. She turned to Lucky. "How was that?"

"That looked really nice, Vida!" Lucky cheered from the fence. She hopped down and ran over to give Cinnamon an oat biscuit. "I think you two might be naturals."

"I want to go again," Vida said, looking at her pocket watch, "but should we get back to start baking?"

"We should get started...." Lucky patted Cinnamon's side. "But I think we have time for one more lap—"

"*Vida Rosales?!*" An excited squeal interrupted them. Lucky knew that voice. She turned around. Sure enough, Maricela stood with her arms crossed and a huge smile on her face. "I hardly recognized you!"

"Maricela Gutierrez?" Vida replied in disbelief. She pulled her boot out from the stirrup and swung her leg down. "Is that you?"

"Who else?" Maricela laughed and put one hand on her hip, as if she were posing. She quickly smoothed her red hair. Lucky frowned. Maricela seemed almost nervous for some reason. "It's *so* good to see you again. What are you doing in Miradero?" Maricela's eyes flicked to Lucky. "Do you two know each other?"

"We're new friends, actually," Vida explained. "I'm just visiting for a few days. Lucky y sus amigas have been helping me learn to ride my new horse." She gestured to Cinnamon. "And in exchange, I'm helping them with their bake sale fund-raiser for the herd they're in. They're going to win a trophy—"

"That is so great," Maricela said through a very fake laugh. Lucky frown deepened. "I have a horse, too, you know! Her name's Mystery. I just *love* riding. I'm even a part of Lucky's herd—the Fearless Fillies—"

"*Frontier* Fillies," Lucky corrected. Why was Maricela lying? Maricela was definitely not into riding horses. She often marched around town, complaining about the mess and the smell. And why was she bothering Vida so much? Maricela was up to something. "How do you two know each other?"

Maricela brushed off her mistake. "Right, that. Vida and I were friends when we were little, before she left Miradero. I haven't seen her since she moved." Maricela turned to smile at Vida. "I hang out with Lucky, Abigail, and Pru *all* the time. We call ourselves the PALMs!" Sometimes,

Maricela liked to add her initial to the end of their group name. But only when it suited her. This wasn't the first time Lucky had heard her make the claim. But it was still odd. She suddenly seemed to be acting like the old Maricela—the snooty version. Lucky didn't like it.

"¿De verdad? I had no idea you were all friends!" Vida replied. She turned back to Maricela. "You should come bake with us. We need all the help we can get!"

Lucky furrowed her brow. She wasn't sure she wanted Maricela's help. She wasn't a Frontier Filly, and she was acting so weird around Vida! On the other hand, Vida seemed so excited to see Maricela. Lucky remembered what Vida's parents had said back at the orchard, about how sad she'd been when she had to move away. Lucky thought of her friends back in the city. If Lucky could spend a few days having fun with them now, she would in a heartbeat. Who was Lucky to get between old friends?

"Okay." Lucky sighed. She forced a polite smile. "But try not to make too much of a mess of things, okay, Maricela?"

Hopefully, the old friendship wouldn't get in the way of the new ones.

Chapter 6

Lucky Prescott's kitchen was a total mess. Again. But this time, the countertops were strewn with all manners of freshly baked apple goodies. The aroma of cinnamon and sugar swirled around the air. The girls had been at it for hours.

As usual, Abigail had acted as head pastry chef. She'd given instructions for Pru to chop apples, for Lucky to mix the dough, and for Vida to help decide which of her family's types of apples went best with which recipe. Before each treat was put into the oven, Abigail would lean down and whisper something to them. "I'm just telling them how yummy they're going to be. It's for good luck!" she explained, as if it were totally normal. Everyone just giggled and shrugged at Abigail's kooky traditions and "secret ingredients."

"What if we used a different fruit than apples?" said Maricela, who was busy cutting out shapes in the dough. "Like a—"

"Then it wouldn't be an *apple* bake sale!" Pru sighed. "We've gotta stick to our theme."

"But there are many autumnal flavors that could satisfy the residents of Miradero. Last year, Cook baked a pumpkin pie that was delectable. I think she still has the recipe! Pumpkin is her *favorite*."

"Maybe next time," Lucky replied, pulling a tray of mini tarts from the oven. Maricela had been making suggestions like this all afternoon. Lucky thought she just wanted to do things *her* way instead of what the PALs and Vida already planned. "We have too much to do already!"

Vida shot Maricela an apologetic look, but she didn't notice it. Maricela looked quite annoyed. She stood up in a huff and offered to be on wash-up duty, which was very unlike her. Lucky was impressed until she saw Maricela constantly turning around to make sure Vida was watching her.

Maricela had washed only four pans and a whisk before complaining that her hands were too delicate to continue. Then she offered to go out front and keep watch on the crates of apples instead. Since they contained the only Rojo Delicioso Orchard apples the girls had, they had to be sure that no horses or sneaky little brothers tried to take them. Maricela invited Vida to go outside with her and reminisce, but Vida was elbows-deep in flour and sugar.

"Not now, Maricela!" Lucky sighed. It was hard enough getting to know Vida with everything they had to do. Maricela trying to hog her was just making it worse! "We need Vida to help us in here!"

Vida tried to smile at Maricela and

promised her that they would catch up about the old days in Miradero later, but Maricela just sighed heavily and left the room.

"Do you think Maricela is okay out there?" asked Vida a few hours later.

"Oh, I'm sure she's fine," Lucky replied. She had lost track of time, but Maricela had to be occupied since she hadn't returned to the kitchen. Lucky wasn't complaining. That girl had a history of complicating even the simplest situations.

"We should open a bakery!" Abigail said proudly. She counted the treats they'd baked so far. They had about six dozen. Only halfway there. "And then after we are a huge success, we can open a bakery exclusively for horses! We could bake my special oat biscuits, oat muffins, oat cookies, oat scones...."

"We kind of *are* opening a bakery," Vida replied. She gestured to all the yummy stuff around them. "A one-day pop-up shop!"

"*Ooooh*, that reminds me!" Abigail

rushed to her cookbook. "We should add apple popovers to the list."

For the rest of the afternoon, the girls kept at it. They stirred.

They mixed. They dreamed up ways to display the Golden Horseshoe (once they won it). It was even more fun than Lucky had anticipated. With the addition of Vida, there were all sorts of new things to talk about. Vida told them all about living in an orchard and taught them little bits of Spanish while Pru, Abigail, and Lucky enjoyed telling Vida everything there was to know about horses. They were deep in a discussion about the difference between a horse's canter and a gallop when Abigail gasped. "Oh no!"

They had completely run out of butter. It was a butter crisis!

"Don't worry, we'll just go get some. We could probably all use a little break anyway," reasoned Lucky. "And we should probably check on the horses when we get back. I bet they're getting hungry for some supper." Abigail and Pru agreed. Vida offered to stay behind and keep chopping the apples.

But when Vida went outside to retrieve another bag of the Granny Smiths for the Apple Abigails, she couldn't find them anywhere. That was odd. Hadn't Maricela offered to watch the crates?

"Maricela?" Vida called out, tiptoeing around the corner of the house. "¿Dónde estás?" She couldn't find Maricela, but she *did* find four burping horses and a pair of practically empty apple crates. The girls weren't close to being done and were completely out of Rojo Delicioso Orchards apples!

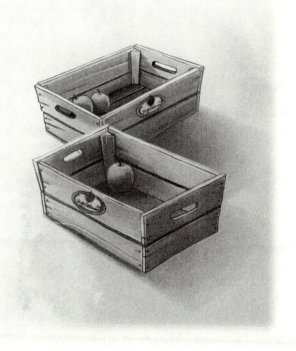

Vida could tell things were about to heat up between her friends, and it wasn't because of the oven.

Chapter 7

Back when Vida lived in Miradero, there hadn't been very many kids in town yet. It was before Hector had even been born! So even though Vida was a couple years older than Maricela, they'd often played together. Being the mayor's daughter, Maricela had always had the nicest toys—a beautiful dollhouse, a wooden rocking horse, and plenty of soft teddy bears. Vida remembered how magnificent Maricela's house was from the long afternoons she'd spent there, so it was easy to spot as she wandered through the center of town.

The huge two-story brick home with the white porch railing looked just the same as Vida remembered. She approached it slowly, feeling a little hesitant. Vida reached out and gingerly knocked on the front door. "Maricela? It's me, Vida."

Vida heard footsteps. The door swung open to reveal Maricela. Vida could just see a woman in an apron peeking out from behind her. Maricela turned around and whispered, "Cook, I'll be back in just a minute! Keep baking, please?"

Maricela stepped outside onto the porch and gestured for Vida to sit. "So nice of you to visit!"

Vida was confused. She wasn't visiting. She was on a mission to find the rest of the apples. "Maybe I've got it all wrong...pero weren't you supposed to be guarding the apple crates?"

"Oh, I was." Maricela laughed. "But it was very boring. And I had a great idea! So I figured I'd just come back later for the part where we get to taste-test everything. Have you come to fetch me for that? I can't wait to show everyone my—"

Vida bit her lip as she cut off Maricela. "No, not quite...."

Maricela was in for a surprise of her own. Delivering bad news was not Vida's strongest suit. She much preferred to be the ray of sunshine in someone's day instead of the cloud. "The rest of the apples are gone. The horses got into them after you left."

If Maricela was shocked, she didn't show it. "Oh, that's why you look so worried?" She waved her hand nonchalantly. "Why don't you just go back to your orchard and get some more?"

"Si, I suppose I could do that. I'll have to wait for Lucky, Pru, and Abigail to come back, though...."

"No, you don't!" Maricela said sharply. "You know the way, right? You and I can just go together! No need to worry our friends about the apples; we'll be back before they even know they're gone!"

"If you're sure...." Vida considered for a moment and nodded. Maricela was right—it would be much quicker for the two of them to head back to the orchard instead of waiting for everyone else to get back first. Plus, Maricela had to be more experienced on horseback than Vida was. If anything went wrong, she'd be in good hands. "You might have to coach me on some of the riding...."

An odd look passed over Maricela's face, but she quickly covered it with a smile. "Of course! I am an excellent rider, but I might take my bicycle this time. Mystery is a bit tired today. She'd probably just slow things down. Let's hurry! We'll be back with those apples before you know it."

Chapter 8

"You'd better be telling the truth!" Abigail warned. She pointed her finger at Snips. Pru and Lucky stood nearby. They were all concerned. When they'd returned with the butter, the PALs had seen that Vida, Maricela, and the apples were all gone, without even a note in their place!

"Relax!" Snips groaned. "Why would I lie about having seen Maricela and that new girl ride away on a horse?"

"Because...because...you're trying to ruin

our Frontier Fillies bake sale, so you can have all the treats for yourself?" As soon as Abigail said the words, she realized how ridiculous she sounded. After the whole incident when Snips had tried to interfere on their behalf so that they could win the Hungerford Heart at the Summer Jamboree, he had stayed far away from all herd activities.

"Not a chance!" Snips laughed. "Besides, Señor Carrots and I are way too busy making stuff for our own booth at the market." He held up a wonky felt carrot with googly eyes. "Stuffed carrot friends! I'm gonna sell 'em for a quarter each. Or gold nuggets, if the customers got 'em!" Señor Carrots, the donkey, snorted his approval.

All this gold-talk made Lucky think about the Golden Horseshoe Trophy, which in turn, made her anxious. Had Vida left to try to get more apples? Why hadn't she waited for Lucky and her friends to return? Had Lucky been so focused on winning the fund-raising contest that Vida thought she had no choice but to go back to the orchard without them?

"Did you see which way they rode?" Lucky pressed. If Maricela and Vida had really gone on a trail ride together, they could be in danger. She knew Maricela didn't know how to ride a horse, and Lucky had only just begun to teach Vida the basics of riding. She would feel awful if her new friend took things too fast. Horses could be unpredictable, especially nervous ones like Cinnamon. Lucky had a very bad feeling in the pit of her stomach, and it wasn't just from all the treats she'd tasted earlier.

Snips pointed. "Definitely that way."

"Thanks, Snips. Come on, girls!" Lucky

called out, taking off toward the stables. "We can finish baking later. We've got to make sure Maricela and Vida are safe first!"

Nobody argued. Pru and Abigail just followed Lucky. Once everyone had mounted their horses, the PALs took off toward their favorite trail. It was the way they had entered

Miradero when they'd brought Vida.

It had been only a few hours since they'd seen Vida, so there was no chance she and Maricela could have made it all the way to the orchard yet. The girls galloped along the stream, searching the landscape as they went. "Maricela! Vida!" they called out, cupping their hands around their mouths. The sound carried through the canyons much better that way.

"Maybe we should split up?" Pru suggested. "We could cover more ground that way."

Lucky shook her head. "No, let's stick together and keep looking. We have to be getting close." The longer they trotted, the worse Lucky began to feel. She was sure the reason Maricela had been acting so weird had something to do with her and Vida's disappearance.

If only Lucky had asked Maricela what was bothering her, none of this would have happened. If only she hadn't worried so much about becoming Vida's friend. They would all be back in her kitchen, finishing up their big baking project. Instead, the sun was starting to set over the horizon. They were running out of time.

Suddenly, Boomerang and Chica Linda began to whinny and stomp. "¡AYUDA!" Vida's voice echoed through the trees. "Help! WE'RE UP HERE!"

Abigail, who had galloped slightly ahead, doubled back. "I see them! They're

stuck on that ledge!" She pointed up. Sure
enough, Maricela and Vida were with
Cinnamon on the narrow, high trail. The
horse whinnied and cried, staring down at
a little break in the path. It was a path for
advanced riders, so there were a few tricky
jumps throughout.

"We're coming!" shouted Lucky. "Don't move a muscle!"

The girls turned their horses around, galloping straight to the trailhead. Boomerang, Chica Linda, and Spirit all knew exactly what to do. The strong horses walked up the path slowly. They didn't want to scare Cinnamon again. The trail was dusty and twisting, so it took them a few minutes to reach the spot.

Finally, the herd arrived. The PALs dismounted from their horses and rushed over to the other girls. "Is anyone hurt?" Pru asked. She always carried extra first-aid supplies with her.

"Nope." Maricela sighed. She looked down at her boots. "Just our pride."

"No entiendo. I don't understand what happened...." Vida shook her head. "Maricela thought this path was a shortcut, but Cinnamon got scared as soon as  he saw the jump. We've been trying to get him to walk back down for an hour, but he won't move!"

"We've all been there," Lucky assured her. There were many times she'd found herself stuck while riding. Her friends had always been there to help her out. "We'll get Cinnamon back down in no time."

It took all five girls and several oat biscuits to coax Cinnamon into turning around. Then they slowly led him down the path by his bridle. The other horses led by example, and Cinnamon seemed to calm down. By the time they'd reached the bottom, it was almost dark out.

"We've got to get home before the sun goes down," Lucky insisted. Riding home in complete darkness was even riskier than a little jump. "We don't want Cinnamon getting spooked again."

"Maricela, you ride your bicycle next to me and Chica Linda," ordered Pru as she climbed up onto the saddle. "We'll go slowly."

The ride home was smooth. But Lucky

knew that as soon as she could manage it, she would have to confront Maricela about what she'd done. Lucky would also have to admit that maybe she had been a little distracted.

That's when things would start to get rocky.

Chapter 9

The next morning, Lucky woke up early.
She was surprised to see that Vida was
already awake. Lucky supposed that life
on the farm had trained Vida to get up
before the sunrise, whether she wanted
to or not. The two girls crept downstairs
through the dark house and found the
kitchen. All the baked goods sat in neat
rows on the table, covered and ready to
go to the market, just as the girls had left
them the previous afternoon. There were

fewer than they had originally planned on, but it would have to do.

They had worked so hard to bake everything for the big sale. As Vida looked at the few treats they had, Lucky could tell she felt really bad about how yesterday had gone. Lucky felt bad about it, too.

"Lo siento. Maricela and I shouldn't have left like that yesterday," Vida said sadly. "I felt so bad about the rest of the apples going missing, and I wanted to fix it. Maricela told me we didn't need to wait for you to get back."

Lucky shook her head. "You don't have to apologize, Vida. In fact, I think I'm the one who should say sorry."

Vida frowned. "Why is that?"

"I got so excited about winning the contest and about having you as a new friend that I was ignoring Maricela's ideas about the bake sale. I think I was a little bit jealous, actually," Lucky admitted. Her cheeks flushed red. "You two were so excited to see each other, but I wanted you to be excited about what we were doing, too! It actually reminds me of one of the first trail rides I ever went on with Pru and Abigail. I kept trying to ask them about riding and Miradero because I was so happy to know them, but Spirit kept whinnying because he wanted attention, too!"

At this, Vida began to giggle. Which, in turn, made Lucky giggle. Finally, Lucky pulled herself together. "Why are we laughing?"

Vida nudged Lucky. "Because it's silly. We can *all* be friends! No competition."

Lucky gestured to all the baked goods. "Other than the fund-raising one...We don't have nearly enough to sell to win the contest." Maybe there was still a chance to come up with a plan. Lucky wasn't sure what that plan would be, but she knew that she was ready to figure out one—with Maricela.

Vida and Lucky quietly left the house and walked down Miradero's peaceful streets. Once they reached the big redbrick house, they were surprised to see Maricela sitting on the porch in her bathrobe.

"Vida! Lucky!" Maricela gasped as if she'd seen a pair of ghosts. She tied her robe around herself tighter. "Why are you here so early?"

"We couldn't sleep," Lucky said. She climbed up the front steps and leaned against the railing. Vida followed.

"Me neither," Maricela admitted, gesturing to her pajamas. She looked really tired.

Vida nodded. "We didn't mean to scare you!"

"You didn't," Maricela lied.

A moment of awkward silence went by before Vida spoke. "So...why did you lie about being part of the Frontier Fillies? Why didn't you say you didn't know how to ride?" She tucked her hair behind her ears and met Maricela's gaze. "Está bien, you can tell us."

"Ugh, *fine*." Maricela glanced over at Lucky and groaned. "If you really want me to admit it, I will. I...wanted to impress you."

"¿Por qué?" Vida asked.

"Why?" Maricela plopped back down

onto the steps. "Because—as embarrassing as this is to admit—I've always looked up to you, Vida. Ever since we were little, you were always the older and cooler girl. Then you moved away. You finally come back, and then Abigail, Pru, and Lucky impress you right away with all that silly horse stuff! I mean, I love Mystery, but I don't know as much as they do about horses."

Vida and Lucky broke into giggles again.

"What's so funny?" Maricela crossed her arms in a huff. Her normally tidy red hair was frizzing out every which way, which made her look even sillier.

"We don't mean to laugh...." Vida nudged Maricela. "But we don't have to try to impress each other. I have always liked you just the way you are. And so do Lucky, Abigail, and Pru!" Vida couldn't believe someone like Maricela would spend so much effort to try to look cool in front of her. "Right, Lucky?"

"That's right." Lucky nodded with a smile. "And I'm sorry I wouldn't listen to your ideas for the bake sale. That wasn't fair."

"Oh, it's okay...." Maricela relaxed. "I'm glad we can still all be friends, even if we acted a bit ridiculous."

The three friends hugged, and Maricela invited Vida and Lucky inside for some tea and breakfast. As they entered the kitchen, Lucky smelled something delicious. There was a tray of a dozen perfect little pies on the counter. Only these pies were a different color than the ones in Lucky's kitchen. These were orange, and each one had a small horseshoe made of crust in the center.

"Wow," Lucky breathed.

Vida inhaled the yummy scents. "Are these baked with—"

"Pumpkin?" Maricela finished the sentence and smiled. "Yes. As I was trying to tell you, it's Cook's favorite. Do you want to try one?"

Maricela reached over, picked the two prettiest pies, and served them on plates for Lucky and Vida. As the girls bit into the buttery crust and creamy pumpkin mixture, they couldn't hide their delight. The pies tasted exactly like autumn, and that gave Lucky an idea.

She knew exactly how they were going to solve the dilemma of the missing apples.

Chapter 10

"So we have good news and we have bad news," Lucky announced. The gang was gathered in Lucky's kitchen, ready to bake the rest of the treats they hadn't gotten to the night before. The Fall Market Festival was set to begin that very afternoon. Maricela stood behind Vida, a sheepish look on her face.

"Give us the bad news first," Pru insisted suspiciously. It was never a good sign when Maricela had that look on her face. "It's always better to end on the good news."

Vida took a deep breath. "So, the horses ate the rest of our special apples. That's why we tried going back to the orchard. We don't have enough to finish baking."

"What?!" Abigail cried out. She pointed to her notebook. "But we didn't even get to make the Apple Abigails! They were going to be delicious little apple dumpling pockets dusted with sugar...."

"I figured something like that might have happened..." Pru said, putting the pieces together. "I knew something was up when I saw Chica Linda's stash of apple cores in the back of her stall."

"Sorry. I know I was supposed to be guarding the apples," Maricela said with a wince. "But I got distracted by an idea and I couldn't wait. At least your horses got to enjoy them?"

"Is that the good news?" Pru retorted.

"No." Vida smiled. "It's much, much better. Come see it for yourself." She led the girls out to the back yard.

Pru and Abigail couldn't believe their eyes! There, in Lucky's yard, stood a beautiful blue wooden cart. It even had a pastry-display cabinet with some treats already inside. The best part was painted on the wagon: the exact logo from Vida's drawing! It had two apples and a golden horseshoe in the center. Below it, in swirly letters, it read: *Miradero Frontier Fillies' Filling Station, featuring Rojo Delicioso*

Orchards Apples (and Pumpkin Treats)

"Wow!" the girls exclaimed, rushing over to check out their new cart. "It's perfect!"

"Maricela, Vida, and I converted her old puppet show wagon into a traveling treat cart!" Lucky said, beaming with pride. "Now we can fund-raise whenever we like. Just bake up some fresh treats and roll the cart around town!"

"That means you'll have to ride Cinnamon out here and visit us," Maricela said, turning to Vida. "So the girls can keep giving you lessons."

"Deal." Vida smiled warmly at Maricela. "I'll bring mi familia next time! How else will you get your shipments of Rojo Delicioso Orchards apples?"

Pru and Abigail were still gawking at the new cart, taking turns rolling it around and shouting "Treats for sale!" to no one in particular. Suddenly, Pru stopped and turned to Maricela. "Hey...where did you get these adorable mini pumpkin pies?"

"I baked them!" Maricela said, turning up her nose. Vida shot her a look. Maricela sighed. She had promised to work on not telling so many little white lies. "I mean... *Cook* baked them. But I did help. The horseshoe decorations were

my extra special touch. After the horses ate the apples, I figured donating some of Cook's pastries to the bake sale was the least I could do."

"Really?" Pru asked in awe. "Well, they look fantastic! I wish we had more of them so we'd have enough for the contest. Maybe even some other pumpkin treats, too—"

"Like pumpkin cupcakes with whipped cream cheese frosting?" Abigail interrupted. The wheels in her head were beginning to turn. "Or sugared pumpkin bread with walnuts?"

"I have an even better idea..." Maricela said, raising a brow.

Everyone braced themselves for her next sassy remark.

"How about *both*?" Maricela finished with a smile. She rolled up her sleeves and a look of determination settled on her face. "If we work together, I'm sure we can get it done!"

That was enough for the PALs. "That's exactly what I was thinking, Maricela." Lucky beamed with pride and cheered. "All right, let's get ready, Fillies. We've got a lot more baking to do and not much time to do it!"

～ Chapter 11 ～

It was a beautiful day on the trails. Lucky, Pru, Abigail, and Maricela had basked in the golden sunshine, taking the trip at an easy pace. But Lucky was eager to get there already. She couldn't wait to see Vida and tell her everything that had happened since their last visit. Of course, Lucky had already written her new friend a letter to tell her the good news. Thanks to Vida (and the amazing treat cart), their bake sale had far exceeded their fund-raising goals.

The Miradero Herd had won the Golden Horseshoe by a landslide!

When they finally crested the familiar hill, Lucky could see the Rojo Delicioso Orchards sign in the distance. "There it is!" Lucky shouted, and Spirit began to pick up his pace to a gallop. He was probably just as excited as she was, having been promised all the apples he could eat.

Boomerang and Chica Linda followed, carrying Abigail, Pru, and Maricela. But the horses didn't even stop to eat any apples. They ran straight to the stable to greet their old friend Cinnamon! The four horses whinnied and kicked, saying hello to one another.

"You're here!" Vida came running out of the barn. "¡Bienvenidos!"

"We've missed you much," Lucky said. She gave Spirit an affectionate pat and let him run off into the orchard. She gave Vida a hug. "And we have so much to tell you. But first, we have something to give you...."

Abigail and Pru stepped forward, smiling. They held something behind their backs. Vida looked confused, but intrigued. "Something to give me?"

"Ta-da!" the girls said in unison as they stepped apart to reveal the one-and-only Frontier Fillies Golden Horseshoe Trophy. It glittered in the sunlight.

"We *were* going to display it in the barn," Lucky explained with a smile, "but we decided that you two deserve it, after everything you did to help us. You and Cinnamon should be the ones to have it."

The girls helped Vida as she lifted the trophy onto the windowsill above Cinnamon's stall. The golden color  shone brightly against the light brown of the wooden planks. It was perfecto. Vida was overwhelmed by the beautiful gift and the thoughtfulness of her new friends.

As the girls visited over slices of Maria's famous apple pie, Lucky felt grateful. It wasn't always about winning golden trophies. Friendship was the sweetest victory of them all. Especially if it included desserts!

G. M. (Gillian) Berrow is also the author of many My Little Pony chapter books and middle-grade novels, including the beloved in-world book series, the Daring Do Adventures. She loves writing about ponies and horses, playing with her mini poodle, and making puns.

Born in La Plata, Argentina, **Maine Diaz** grew up drawing and painting. Cartoons captured her imagination early on, and she realized immediately that she wanted to be an animator when she grew up. At the age of sixteen, Maine took a workshop and started animating. Soon after, she started illustrating for children's storybooks and educational books.

Currently, Maine lives in a tiny green house, where she spends time with her two cats, Chula and Lola. When not illustrating, she enjoys swimming, writing, and taking photos.

Calling All Horse Lovers!

Explore the world of DreamWorks Animation's
Spirit Riding Free **with this adventurous series**
featuring the innermost thoughts of your favorite PALs!

Share your thoughts using #ReadSpirit